My First Book of Nature

I0808666

Birds

Victoria Munson

WINDMILL BOOKS

Published in 2019 by Windmill Books,
an Imprint of Rosen Publishing
29 East 21st Street, New York, NY 10010

Copyright © 2019 Wayland, a division of
Hachette Children's Group

All rights reserved. No part of this book may be reproduced in any form without permission in writing from the publisher, except by a reviewer.

Editor: Victoria Brooker
Book Design: Elaine Wilkinson

Photo Credits:
All graphics Shutterstock.com, and cover: main Mark Medcalf tr Menno Schaefer; tl Alexander Erdbeer; bl Jozef Sowa; br Cric Isselee; 1, 6 Edwin/Butter/; 4 Dominique de La Croix; 5t ChameleonsEye; 5b dmodlin01; 6b Howard Marsh; 7t Bruce MacQueen; 7b RT Images; 8l Marc Goldman; 8r John Navajo; 9t Bildagentur Zoonar GmbH; 9b Visayas; 10l Zakharov Aleksey; 10r FotoRequest; 11 Rudmer Zwerver; 12 Belen Bilgic Schneider; 13t Arvind Balaraman; 13b Juan Roballo; 14t MAC1; 14b Paul Cummings; 15t V. Belov; 16 Chris Hill; 17t Mark Medcalf; 17b Tobyphotos; 18 Jack53; 19 Michal Ninger; 20 Rafal Szozda; 21t Bildagentur Zoonar GmbH; 21b Drakuliren; 11, 19t istock by Getty Images

Cataloging-in-Publication Data

Names: Munson, Victoria.
Title: Birds / Victoria Munson.
Description: New York : Windmill Books, 2019. | Series: My first book of nature | Includes glossary and index.
Identifiers: LCCN ISBN 9781508196600 (pbk.) | ISBN 9781508196594 (library bound) | ISBN 9781508196617 (6 pack)
Subjects: LCSH: Birds--Juvenile literature.
Classification: LCC QL676.2 M86 2019 | DDC 598--dc23

Manufactured in the United States of America

CPSIA Compliance Information: Batch #BS18WM:
For Further Information contact Rosen Publishing,
New York, New York at 1-800-237-9932

Contents

What Is a Bird?

Birds are warm-blooded animals that can lay eggs. A bird has feathers and wings. No other animal has feathers. Birds have a beak but no teeth.

Feathers are used to keep birds warm, help them to fly, and provide camouflage.

Most birds can fly. However, there are some birds that don't. These include penguins, ostriches, and kiwis.

Penguins are very strong swimmers, and ostriches are fast runners.

Penguins live at the cold South Pole.

Ostriches can run at 60 mph (97 km/h)!

Birds are found all over the world. Parrots are found in hot rainforests.

Flamingos live together in large groups near lakes and swamps.

Backyard Birds

Robins are small birds with bright red breasts. They love to sing from early in the morning to late at night.

Robins eat apples, nuts, and even spiders.

Male blackbirds have a bright yellow-orange beak.

Blackbirds eat worms, berries, and fruit.

Mourning doves lay two eggs at a time. They can lay eggs up to six times a year. That's twelve baby mourning doves a year!

Mourning doves make sad cooing sounds.

Juncos are snowbirds. They like winter!

Juncos can be gray and white or reddish brown. They look for food by hopping and walking along the ground.

City Birds

Male house sparrows have a black head and neck with white cheeks. Female sparrows are brown with no black markings.

Sparrows are very common in towns and cities.

Magpies are large **black and white birds.**

Magpie nests sometimes have roofs and two entrances. They have a loud chattering call.

chatter

chatter

Starlings live together in large flocks. A group of starlings is called a chattering.

Pigeons are the most common city bird. They are gray with shades of green and purple on their neck.

Starlings are very good at copying the sound of other birds, mammals, or even telephones!

Ring! Ring!

Pigeons live in large groups to protect themselves from predators such as cats, foxes, and rats.

Forest Birds

Song thrushes have heart-shaped brown spots on their cream-colored breasts. Mistle thrushes look very similar but are slightly larger.

Blue jays have bright blue feathers, white bellies, and pointy crests on their heads.

Blue jays are one of the loudest birds. Their call sounds like "Jay! Jay!"

Great spotted woodpeckers are black and white with a red patch under their tail.

Woodpeckers have two toes facing forward and two facing backwards.

Nuthatches are small, colorful birds with blue-gray wings and orange-brown breasts.

Nuthatches have a thick black line over each eye. Look for them walking upside down on hazel and beech trees.

Water Birds

Mallards live all over North America, Europe, and Asia. Male mallards have a green head, yellow beak, and white ring around their neck. Female mallards are speckled brown.

Don't feed ducks bread. It is bad for them. Instead, feed them seeds and berries.

Swans are very large white birds.

Swans have a long "S"-shaped neck. When angry, they will hiss and flap their wings.

Young swans are called cygnets.

Canada geese have long black necks and white cheeks. Large flocks of geese group together in parks and fields.

Look up to see these geese flying by in a "V" shape.

Canada geese can fly at 18 mph (30 km/h).

Moorhens are black with a red forehead. They live in ponds, rivers, and lakes. Their long green toes help them to grip on wet stones.

Coots look similar to moorhens, but they have a white forehead and beak. Coots can run along the surface of water.

Seabirds

Herring gulls are large, noisy birds. They have a red spot on their curved yellow beaks. When hungry chicks peck the red spot on the adult's beak, the adult knows to open its mouth and give food to its young.

In summer, black-headed gulls have black heads. For the rest of the year, their head has brown stripes. They like to live in groups.

Gulls eat fish, worms, and insects.

Oystercatchers have black and white bodies with long, bright orange beaks. They use their long beaks to open mussel shells.

Puffins live in groups on cliffs. They are black and white with a very colorful curved beak and bright orange legs.

Puffins eat tiny silver fish called sand eels.

Birds of Prey

Adult bald eagles have a dark brown body, and a white head and tail.

Eagles have a huge wingspan of over 6 feet (2 m).

Eagles have long, sharp talons for grabbing their prey.

Birds of prey sometimes perch on telephone poles along the road.

Sparrowhawks have a bar pattern across their chest. They do not hover like kestrels, but fly quickly, looking for small birds to eat.

The sparrowhawk's hooked beak helps it to scoop up prey.

Kestrels are small birds of prey with a long tail and pointed wings.

They hover above the ground before swooping down on their prey.

Kestrels eat small mammals such as mice and voles.

Owls

Barn owls have a snowy white breast and honey-colored back and wings. Their white face is heart-shaped.

Owls are *usually* nocturnal, which means they hunt at night, but barn owls can sometimes be seen in the daytime.

Look for barn owls in the early evening perched by the road. They are waiting to swoop down and catch mice and voles.

Long-eared owls are light brown with dark brown streaks. They get their name from their long ears! They have a dark brown, round face with orange eyes.

The male's loud hoot can be heard up to half a mile (1 km) away.

Hooot!

Short-eared owls have a brownish-black body, white face, and yellow eyes. Owls swallow their prey whole.

Short-eared owls can be seen hunting in the daytime.

Country Birds

Pheasants have long, beautiful tail feathers. Males are dark golden brown with a green head and red face wattles.

Females are paler brown and black. Pheasants live in fields.

Pheasants have excellent sight and hearing, which they use to help them avoid predators, such as foxes and birds of prey.

Redwings look like thrushes but have a bright red patch under their wings and a yellow stripe above their eyes.

In the fall, redwings fly in flocks of hundreds of birds.

Gray partridges have an orange face and mottled gray feathers. Their wings make a loud whirring noise when they fly.

Gray partridges lay one of the largest clutches of eggs in the world – 15 to 19 per nest!

Follow That Footprint

Sometimes it's hard to spot animals. Find out if a bird has been nearby by looking for clues.

Duck

In soft mud, birds will leave footprints behind.

Crow

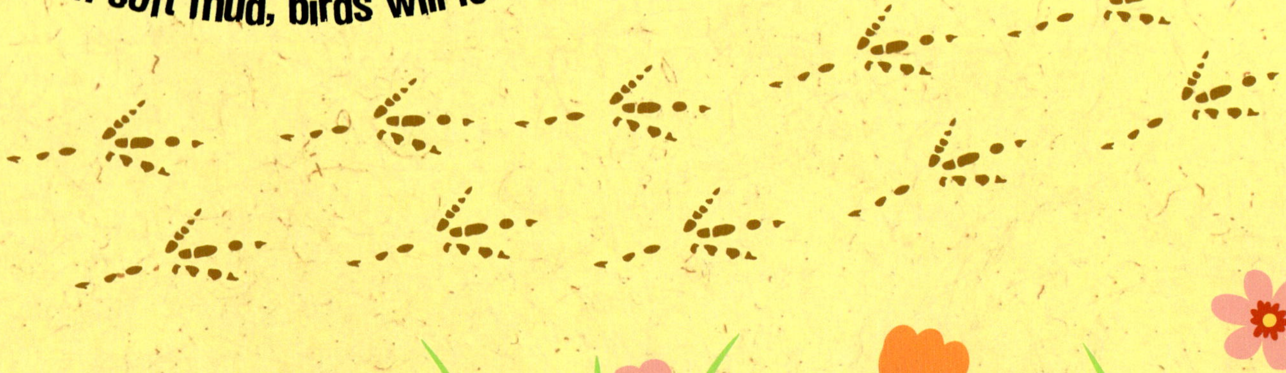

Look at these footprints and see
if you can spot any in your local wildlife habitat.
Moorhen
Bird of prey

Glossary and Index

camouflage colors on an animal's body that blend with the background, making it difficult to spot

predator an animal that hunts, kills, and eats other animals

prey an animal that is hunted and killed for food for another animal

warm-blooded having a body temperature that remains steady and warm, no matter what the outside temperature is. Mammals and birds are warm-blooded animals.